First published in Great Britain in 1989 by Hutchinson Children's Books
An imprint of Century Hutchinson Ltd
Brookmount House, 62-65 Chandos Place,
Covent Garden, London WC2N 4NW

Century Hutchinson Australia (Pty) Ltd
88-91 Albion Street, Surry Hills, NSW 2010

Century Hutchinson New Zealand Ltd
32-34 View Road, PO Box 40-086, Glenfield, Auckland 10

Century Hutchinson South Africa (Pty) Ltd
PO Box 337, Bergvlei 2012, South Africa

Printed and bound in Belgium

British Library Cataloguing in Publication Data
Weevers, Peter
The march hare.
I. Title II. Bush, John
821′914

ISBN 0-09-173603-X

Peter Weevers
The March Hare
and other poems

Poems by John Bush

Hutchinson
London   Sydney   Auckland   Johannesburg

Teacher Tobias

Softly, softly the slow sun sinks
And paints the sky in golds and pinks.
What a day! Me oh my!
Thinks Tobias, with a sigh.

Been on the hop since he woke,
Teaching toadlings how to croak,
How to dive, how to swim
And how to hold a deep breath in.

Softly, softly the first star winks;
Two tired eyes give two tired blinks.
Tobias's thoughts turn to sleeping;
Tomorrow he's teaching lilypad leaping.

Badger's Song

Badger's a fellow of quiet, shy way,
Who's seldom about by the light of day,
But come the night, from his burrow he scurries
And off on a badgery jaunt he hurries.

With waddling walk he roams and roves,
Searching for titbits in meadows and groves.
And while the crickets chirp along,
In badgery voice he sings his song:

'Oh I would nothing but a badger be,
Oh a badger's ways are the ways for me.
In a badger's life I do delight,
Stay home all day, stay out all night!'

Harvest Mouse Holidays

Nicholas harvest mouse plays and swings
On a stalk of wheat as it sways, and sings
A summer's song on a summer's breeze,
That tickles his whiskers and rustles the leaves.

He's wished and wished, and waited all year
For the harvest holidays to be here.
Now summer's promise is kept at last;
'Oh please,' cries Nick, 'don't go *too* fast!'

Holiday time means time to play
From dawn to dusk, every day!
New adventures each afternoon
And bedtimes blest by the harvest moon.

Marcel the Fisherman

Oh who knows the run of the river as well
As the water-vole fisherman named Marcel?
There's not an angler half as good,
From winding bank to way-off wood.

Marcel can tell when a day's just right.
He can just sense that the fish will bite.
Is it the touch of the breeze on his nose,
Or a special feeling he gets in his toes?

On such a day, his basket he'll pack,
And set off wearing his luckiest hat.
And each time he does, he secretly wishes,
That this time he'll catch the biggest of fishes.

The March Hare and the Moon

How the March Hare loves a night
When the moon shines full and bright,
And the sounds of summer fill the air,
And it feels so good to be a March Hare.

As the moon begins to climb,
The March Hare sits him down to dine
On a feast of berries, deliciously ripe,
And a pint of ale in the pale moonlight.

And as the moon climbs higher still,
Hare lays back on a grassy hill.
His whiskers twitch as he hops and plays
In enchanting dreams of bygone days.

Reverend Bartholomew Mole

Reverend Bartholomew sniffs the dawn,
Rich with the scents of a summer's morn.
He sniffs again, then stops to say,
'Smells like another perfect day!

'Well, mustn't dawdle, mustn't stop,
Must be off to tend my flock.
So much to do, so many to see,
But first, perhaps, a cup of tea.'

The kettle boils, the tea is made,
And sipped with toast and marmalade.
Then as the new day's sunlight falls,
Bartholomew shuffles off on his calls.

Of Rainbows and Rose Hips

A shower of rain has washed the sky;
A rainbow's arc sweeps up high.
On leaftips, drops like pearls of glass
Gather and fall to jewel the grass.

Lucinda bank vole scuttles about,
Taking her chance now the sun is out,
Collecting up her favourite treat,
Bright red rose hips, juicy and sweet.

She'll take as many as she can store,
Sometimes five, or even more.
And in her pantry they will stay,
Saved up for a rainy day.

Mary Jane Dreams

Beneath a warm and sun-soaked sky,
Mary Jane so quiet and shy,
Daydreams as she blissfully eats
Of summer's green and luscious treats.

Dreams of golden, dandelion days;
Dreams of a rabbit's carefree ways;
Of meadows that stretch too far to hop;
Of summers that come and never stop.

Dream, Mary Jane, for seasons are fleeting,
And youth, like summer, has no keeping.
Dream, Mary Jane, whatever you will,
And always remember when time stood still.

Crafty O'Farley

Who goes by in his red chequered cap?
'Tis crafty O'Farley, that roguish chap;
A raggedy, rambling, rascally sort,
Whose motto is: 'Stolen's better than bought.'

Scruffy scoundrel, you're still on the run,
Shoes worn through and, as always, undone.
Are you planning your next tasty meal?
Whose plump chickens or ducks will you steal?

So far your cunning's been more than a match
For hound and for gun, for lock and for latch.
You may say, 'Stolen's better than bought.'
But others say, 'Show me the thief who's not caught.'

Fulbert the Gourmet

Beside a grassy river bank, bathed in evening's
  glow,
The river's mirror ripples, ruffled by a toe.
Fulbert smiles the drowsy smile of one who is
  replete;
One last drop of raspberry wine and supper is
  complete.

'The richness of this evening was matched in full,
  I feel,
By the succulence and savour of a very splendid
  meal.
The waterlily soup was fine, the dragonflies
  delicious,
As was the walnut trifle, not to mention most
  nutritious.

'These buttons on my waistcoat say perhaps it's time
  to diet,
But frankly I love food too much, oh *far* too much
  to try it!
And anyway, in all my days, I have never found
A frog whose form was ever any better shape than
  round.'

Quentin Owl Waits

In fading twilight, perched in his pine,
Quentin owl sits, dressed up to dine,
A table awaits at the Willow and Nook,
Reserved for himself and Lyle the rook.

'I wonder,' he mumbles, 'why Lyle's so late?
He said he'd be here by a quarter past eight.
Mind you, he's never paid much heed to time.
Oh well, I'll wait, but only till nine.

'I'm feeling quite peckish. Where *are* you Lyle?
It's rude to make friends wait such a long while!
I should think a good subject for dinner debate
Would be the wisdom of not being late.'

Rathbold Reflects

Of all the evenings there've ever been,
This one's as fine as any I've seen.
Not a breath of wind to be felt on the hair,
Just look how the twilight hangs in the air.'

Rathbold leans lazily back on a tree,
Enjoying the balmy tranquillity.
It's been years since he and his wife
Left the city for the woodland life.

'So glad,' says Rathbold, 'we made the change,
I always found the city strange.
Some say there's more to do and see,
But the woodland life is the life for me.'